BY THE SEA

Mary Hofstrand

Puffin Books

PUFFIN BOOKS

Published by the Penguin Group

Viking Penguin, a division of Penguin Books USA Inc.,

40 West 23rd Street, New York, New York 10010, U.S.A.

Penguin Books Ltd, 27 Wrights Lane, London W8 5TZ, England

Penguin Books Australia Ltd, Ringwood, Victoria, Australia

Penguin Books Canada Ltd, 2801 John Street, Markham, Ontario, Canada L3R 1B4

Penguin Books (N.Z.) Ltd, 182–190 Wairau Road, Auckland 10, New Zealand

Penguin Books Ltd, Registered Offices: Harmondsworth, Middlesex, England

First published in the United States of America by Atheneum,
a division of Macmillan Publishing Company, 1989
Published in Picture Puffins, 1990
1   3   5   7   9   10   8   6   4   2

LIBRARY OF CONGRESS CATALOGING-IN-PUBLICATION DATA
Hofstrand, Mary.   By the sea / Mary Hofstrand.   p.   cm.
Summary: A young pig relates how his daily routine changes when
his parents take him to the seashore.
ISBN 0-14-054208-6
[1. Seashore—Fiction.   2. Parent and child—Fiction.   3. Pigs—
Fiction.   4. Stories in rhyme.]   I. Title.
[PZ8.3.H686By   1990]   [E]—dc20   89-36028

Printed in Hong Kong
Set in Caslon 540

For John and Julie

At home I wear shoes and suspenders.

At home I take naps until three.

But when we go down to the seaside,

I'm always just me by the sea.

I sit in the sand
With my bucket in hand,

I don't have to come in for tea.

And I seldom wear clothes,
Because everyone knows,

I'm always just me by the sea.

At home Mama's always too busy.

She says, "Maybe later," to me.

But when we go

down to the seaside,

She's always with me by the sea.

She chases the waves.

She makes castles and caves.

She strolls with me out to the quay.

If we go for a ride,
She laughs by my side.

She's always with me by the sea.

At home Papa's always too busy.

He says, "Maybe next time," to me.

But when we go

down to the seaside,

It's always we three by the sea.

He tosses me up.

He puts shells in my cup.

We all have a holiday spree.

And we don't go to bed,

We watch rockets instead,

For it's always we three by the sea.